Beyond the Wall of Sleep

BEYOND THE WALL OF SLEEP

A COLLECTION OF
PROSE AND POETRY
1988 – 1997

by

R. ANDREW HEIDEL

MORTCO
P.O. Box 1430
Cooper Station
New York, NY 10276

Library of Congress Catalog Card Number: 98-91591
ISBN: 0-9665224-0-0

Exclusive Christmas Printing: December 1997

First MORTCO Printing: September 1998

Printed in the U.S.A.

"You may take what is yours,
return what was borrowed, and bring
upon yourself what is to come.
There is no understanding life.
Only living."

for me

Table of Contents

PROSE

Dead Drunk

Staring Skyward

The God Makers

Faith

Solace

Ava Bryne

Interview with God

The Dead Travel Fast

The Voice

POETRY

THE PROSE

DEAD DRUNK

I was drunk with Death. She had been drinking heavily for the past three hours when I found her at the Slaughtered Lamb Pub. Five shot glasses and miscellaneous condensation rings were scattered about her like a shaman's chicken bones.

No one dared approach her, they knew her task intuitively. Everyone in that bar was soberly reminded of their own mortality, even the dark mahogany walls. It was as if today were April 16 and they had forgotten to file their income tax returns. A man in a grey overcoat checked his date book nervously. It was only February 29. Plenty of time, or so it seemed.

As I approached Death, I noticed her eyebrows were heavy with thought and confusion. The two brows, slender as caterpillars, were pushing forward the small tuft of skin known as the "puzzlement zone."

I had met Death once before. She had visited me as a child when I had a very bad accident involving chicken wire and a friend's golf club. She stood before me with open arms like my mother greeting me from school. Her eyes were full of understanding for the suffering on Earth. She was so beautiful and I wanted nothing else but to know her embrace, to hold me until the hurt of the world went away. The hurt went away because she took you from this world. But the arms of modern science and ancient prayer were longer and stronger. They kept me in this world. I lived.

1

I took the empty barstool to her left. "Would you mind some company?" I ventured.

Death rubbed a shapely and tapered reed-like finger around the rim of a shot glass. She would have been a good pianist, I thought. Her finger stopped twirling and she replied in the lonesome voice of a cattail, "No, not at all."

I caught the eye of the bartender, Sally. She was curious to see who sat with Death. When she realized I was looking at her and wanted service, she cursed herself for looking in the first place. It was spooky enough serving Death when she was sitting by herself, thought the bartender, but now Death had a friend, too! Who else would drop by? What sort of mess would they make if they all got really drunk? Curiosity killed the cat, chimed into her head. The only thing that kept Sally serving up drinks was the thought that the supernatural must tip well. At least she remembered one of her friends mentioning that. "What can I get you?" asked Sally sweetly, as nervous tension made her sweat profusely.

I pointed down at the empty shot glasses with the peace hand signal. "Two more of the same," I requested. It amazes me how much sign language is used at restaurants. To gain a waiter's attention, I look in his direction. If I want the check, I make a writing gesture in the air. More water? I pretend to drink from an invisible glass. It also amazed me that I was about to talk to Death while stone sober — granite from New Hampshire, that is. I gently removed my thumb from my third finger and pinkie, letting those two pink and pudgy digits join their mates and ostracize my thumb in the palm of my hand. "Better make that four."

Death grinned, but the outskirts of her pale smile were marshes where sorrow nested. "Drinking with Death is not always the grandest of ideas," she began.

Nor is playing fiddle against the devil, I thought.

"But I would like your company. And the Jameson whisky should help keep your fragile mind from hemorrhaging with the reality of conversing with me."

Sally was almost finished pouring the shots with a shaky hand. "Why are you here?" I asked Death. Unfortunately, Sally thought the question was posed at her. She missed the last shot glass and backed away with a worried expression. Had I been with anyone else I would have called her back to apologize. But then again, Death is no one else. Death is herself. Strong yet gentle, a tour guide to the underworld. I imagined what the tour must be like.

*"Over here on the left are the gates of
Hades; please, no flash photography, it will
incite Cerebus to attack. Oh, Mrs. Jacobs,
please watch your step, the precipice is
precarious. Now up ahead to the right you
can just barely make out the form of Sisyphus
pushing his rock up the hill. Oh dear, he lost
his grip again. Look out Mr. Goldberg!"*

I picked up a shot of the Irish elixir and brought it to my lips in a lay-up motion. The 80 proof fluid glided over my taste buds, rebounded off the backboard of my throat, and slid right down. "Score!" sounded my uvula who witnessed the entire play. The whiskey warmed my belly immediately like the fear of an oncoming car.

"I can't do it anymore," Death began with a pleading voice. "I am tired and as old as when life first appeared." Death took a breath, she looked as if she wanted to smoke a cigarette. "Being immortal has its drawbacks, the most important of them being I have no one, no one, to share time with. Keeping everything I have done, seen and experienced to myself is killing me; so to speak. There has to be more to existence, even my existence, than this aeon of loneliness."

I had been rolling the empty shotglass back and forth between my palms in my lap. I realized this must appear very suggestive so I placed it among the others on the bar. "Couldn't you talk to God or something?"

We were now taking turns drinking. In one deft movement, Death snatched the shot she had been watching, held it lovingly between her hands and drank it slowly, enjoying every last drop she drew from the vessel. Had I attempted the same maneuver, I would have gagged on the alcohol. Death didn't even wince. She had tasted the life of billions upon billions and enjoyed them all. Stars were juicy, ripe as peaches hanging from the Yggdrasil in Odin's orchard. Planets, being crunchy, made up a solar trail mix: they helped to keep her going. But humans? Humans, each one a special savory treat. Their souls mingled with their life force, seasoning it with the style of lives they had led. Making a visit to a natural disaster site was like ordering out Chinese food for Death. Sweet and sour people, some hot and spicy, others lo mien, and the ones who did nothing with their life were like raw tofu.

The only time Death remembers wincing was when she took the life-force of Hitler during one of his many incarnations. He was not a pleasant sour like that of very tart homemade lemonade; Hitler's life tasted more like rancid low-fat strawberry Dannon Yogurt eaten with a spoon made of tinfoil. This was not a pleasant experience. Death just had to keep him down long enough until she made it to hell's lavatory.

Hell's lavatory by the way is not a pleasant olfactory experience. Suffice to say that it smells similar to a men's college dorm bathroom which still has not been cleaned after the big party night. And the heat, as usual, is on full blast baking the urine into a thin yellow crust.

"I saw God earlier today," said Death. "That's why I'm here now." She set her empty vessel back down. Not even a hint of fluid, a micro-milliliter, remained at the bottom. She must have used her tongue but I never saw it. Not even when she spoke. Her half moon lower lip and venusian landscaped upper lip would open and close, purse and pull back, but I never saw a tongue behind those pink satellites.

"God denied you? Doesn't it think you are doing a good job? I mean, you must have been employed for quite some time now. You would think some sort of vacation would be in order, or at least a Christmas bonus."

"God doesn't believe in vacations and it certainly doesn't believe in Christmas. In fact, God doesn't believe in anything anymore."

I couldn't believe what I just heard. I needed support from my new friend Jameson, but I slam dunked him too hard into my mouth. The drink rebounded off the roof of my mouth onto my tongue caught unawares and my taste buds reacted vehemently before Jameson made his way down my throat. I gritted my teeth and forced the whiskey from coming back on court. "What do you mean by that?" I managed to say hoarsely.

"When I saw God this morning I explained to it how tired I was and how I wanted a rest from immortality. But God looked at me very sadly and said that it had grown very tired, too. When God first appeared out of chaos, it found itself alone with its consciousness. God wanted answers as to why it was there and what it was. So God, with the mind of a child, imagined a universe in which to play. And it became so. God then took a part of itself and placed it in the universe so God could play and by playing come to understand itself. You see, the universe is nothing more than God's sand box in which you live.

"God hoped to find answers through all of its independent experiences. Unfortunately, God's highest hope, mankind, turned out to be a bit of a bust. Great achievements? Sure. But most people were afraid to discover the real truths, the truths and mysteries that remained within themselves. Most of mankind was happy to glorify the truths and mysteries that one man discovered more than two thousand years ago, but the worst insults to God were the churches erected in "his" name and which continued to impose "his" divine law the whole world over. Witnessing this stubborn indisposition to change or growth in the western world has been destroying God for quite some time.

"When I appeared, God saw an answer."

I fell off my stool with an audible Thunk!

"You're telling me that God wanted to die?" I couldn't comprehend the ramifications of such a possibility.

"Yes."

.

. . .

?

I placed my hands over my face and smelled the sweet apple scent of Sarah's hair. Sarah! I remembered why I had come to find Death, it was for Sarah. That would come soon. I did not want Sarah to suffer anymore. I needed to calm down and another drink to help me do it. I reached for the bulge in my back pocket. To me it was my wallet, but to Sarah it was my "Butt tumor," although the only time it was ever malignant was when I had an overdue Visa bill. Pulling two twenties from my growth, I waved them in the direction of the bartender. She pretended not to notice out of her peripheral vision. I waved them again until they made the sound of a mallard drake trying to impress a female, and then set them down hoping the endeavor was fruitful. "So?" I asked.

"No one can refuse God, not even I. I brought

God into my arms and God let go of the universe it knew. I am left alone to my own devices now. There is no one making sure I am performing my duty, so why do it? If I refuse to take life from the body, humans shall gain immortality."

"You're wrong!" I yelled at Death. I was upset at her lack of compassion or understanding of the real issue.

"What do you mean?"

"You may be able to grant immortality by denying death to humans, but you do not grant perpetual youth. When you refuse to take life you upset the balance which God created and still exists. You will lock people in their decaying bodies forever. Imagine feeling every fiber of your physical body decay and unravel over the centuries. I am here to plead with you to return to your duty because my wife Sarah lies in agony. She should have died already, along with countless others at the hospital. She prays for death because the pain is so great. But you didn't answer her prayers." I was crying now and had unintentionally taken Death's left hand in my own. Surprisingly, it was warm.

"I will do no such thing. God has abandoned the both of us. I have no further obligation to the human race or to you." She gently removed my hand from hers.

"No! You don't understand. You're sentencing us to immortality in stagnation."

"Isn't lack of change the same as death?" she asked.

I couldn't answer her. "Then the human race has been dead for quite some time," she finished.

Four more shots of Jameson's bloomed as magically as the forty dollars disappeared. Neat trick, I thought. But then again, I wasn't paying much attention to what was going on around me. I drank two shots, one right after the other. This was the strength I needed. My own personal go-juice, or was it for courage considering what I was about to propose to Death.

"Can I take your place?" I stuttered.

Death looked up from her hands, her expression almost happy. "What?"

"Can I take your place?" I felt good that I did not stutter this time. "I am not about to abandon the human race to oblivon. Oblivion, I mean." The alcohol was dribbling my tongue and I felt foolish that what could be my last words were flawed.

"You would do that for me?" asked Death.

"No, I would do it for Sarah."

Death paused for a second time that evening. "Hold me," she said, holding out her long arms toward me.

I held her. Held her tight. I was drunk with death. I tasted her as I took her life, it was bittersweet like Hershey's cocoa. Death collapsed.

I was Death now. I could feel it in the tapestry I had just been woven into.

I found Sarah that evening in a hospital bed, praying for me. I went to her, held her tight, and tasted her life.

It was sweet.

Staring Skyward

Staring skyward,
communing with something celestial, people stopped what
they were doing all over the city.

I saw them everywhere that day. One woman was
at a street corner, eyes vacant, but with a face that was so
alive I began to cry for the joy she was experiencing. She
glowed with a special knowledge. Another man, late in his
years, dropped his cane that appeared to support the
majority of his mass and stood weightless for a spell.
Everything old and tired beneath him, his real spirit above.
What was happening? Is this a mass hallucination or judgment day and if it is judgment day, how come everyone
was seeing angels and none were speaking to me? Was I
forgotten? Or spared?

I had once believed that angels were to be found
everywhere, usually sneaking into a stranger to say a few
words which would have the uncanny ability to stick in
my mind and redirect my life. My last encounter was with
a bumbling drunk who was completely beyond all rational
thought that didn't concern a half pint. I was walking
down 11th avenue toward Denny Way, fretting over my
job as a janitor, the status involved, and not doing anything that involved my two favorite loves: media and food.
And although it shouldn't have mattered that I was clean-
ing toilets for a living, it did. As I passed, he said, "It isn't
what you do but how you do it."

I guess more than anything an encounter with an

angel alters your perception, and an altered perception changes the way you live your life.

But why wasn't I being consulted by the heavenly hosts? I passed a couple holding hands so tight their knuckles were white, but their faces communicated everything to the contrary of the pain they should have been feeling. I thought I had felt alone before. Not having anyone to share things with, grow old with, see things with; but that feeling of alone was nothing compared to how I felt now. Everyone shared a secret that I was not a part of. When the world is against you, nobody is with you. And when God forgets you, you are truly alone.

"Be patient," I told myself. "There are over five billion people in this world and it's going to take a little time to talk to everyone. Plus, you don't even know what is going on. It might just be some mass hallucination. Did you drink tap water today? I didn't think so. There you go. A rational explanation." But it was far from rational for me. The sky was pregnant with angels communicating with everyone but me.

I continued on my way to work: too lost in my thoughts to go anywhere else and too afraid to go home and turn on the news. Throughout the city, people of glass surrounded me, miniature replicas of the towers above me. Skyscrapers I thought. These people have become skyscrapers, running their fingers along that part of the sky where it turns blue.

I found my building deserted; no work to be done. No one to call. Couldn't if I tried — the lines were dead. Too much. I ran for the stairs. I had to shake

someone from their cosmic stupor and make them tell me
what was going on. Outside the front door I found a man
in a suit looking very much like the rest of the people in
the city.

"Hello. Hello. Pardon me but would you mind
telling me what's going on?" No response so I violated the
man's personal space, stood on my tiptoes and screamed in
his face. "HELLO! WHAT THE HELL IS GOING
ON?!"

"Don't you hear them?" he said in a warm, loving
voice without changing his posture or his adoring gaze.
"Don't you hear the Words? The WORDS. They are so
beautiful. I understand. I understand it all and I understand what is to happen."

"What's going to happen?" I demanded, shaking
his shoulders and wishing I could slap that shit-eating grin
off his face.

"Don't you know? Haven't you heard the words?"

"NO! I haven't heard the f. u. c. k. i. n. g. words.
It appears that everyone is hearing them but me, and it
seems like some kind of conspiracy of hope that's making
me desperate."

"I'm sorry you don't understand."

"I don't need your sympathy, I need a fucking clue
as to what's going on here!"

"I can't help you understand. When they choose
to, they will communicate with you. Until then . . . ."

"Until then?" I screamed at the man, sending spit-
tle across his face. "Until then what? Take a crap? Go out
and have myself a nice dinner? What?"

Beyond the Wall of Sleep

It was then that I witnessed the most beautiful event of my life. The man who was standing before me began shimmering with a blue light. His entire body took on an ethereal quality as the glow increased to a brilliant light. I shaded my eyes from a blinding flash, and when I withdrew my hand from my face, he was gone. Up and down the street it looked like people were exploding. Little human flashbulbs, glimmering in blue and then turning to a brilliant light which flashed when they disappeared.

So now I sit in my dark office, staring out the window. There are still a few flashes across the city and the sound, latecomers I presume. The presumption gives me some hope but not much. To help me sort things out, I tell myself the story again for the fourth time.

Staring skyward, communing with something celestial, people stopped what they were doing all over the city to hear the word of God.

I saw them ev . . e . . . r

I understand, and it is beautiful.

The God Makers

Tralgar looked up at the sky; it was a faint blue with high clouds that diffused the light of the sun overhead. He did not understand why the sun moved the way it did. Rising over one part of the land and setting over the water. It made no sense to him, but it still happened day after day. He continued to mend his net with a bone needle and sinew; the work was meditative. In and out, around and around, he would hold the salty twine between his teeth and grind whenever he finished a section and had to tie it off.

Tralgar knew the waters of this area well, better than most of his clan. His daily catch would sometimes double that of most other fishers in the village. Why? He didn't know. Just an inkling of where the fish must be and an inherent luck to fish the right spot. What others claimed to be his great skill Tralgar passed off as his good fortune.

"Good Fortune." The words were new to his vocabulary. In fact, he had to invent them and explain them to his clan so that they could better understand. He explained it to them in terms of a gift.

"I fish where I feel the fish are swimming in great numbers. My catch is great and to me that is a gift, just as if I gave to you one of my herd, that would be a gift. Now if you did not know it was I who gave you one of my herd and you looked upon your own and noticed it had been

14

increased by one, this would be good fortune."

"But who gives to you the gift of the fish?" asked Hogthrax, a strong ox of a man, who carried the same odor as one.

Tralgar had not thought this far yet. Good fortune seemed enough of an explanation to himself while he was in his boat alone. But now, due to his own simple logic, it stood to reason it must be more than that. If it were a gift, from whom would it come. "The sea gives the gift of the fish." It seemed logical. Who else had the fish to give?

"You must have befriended the sea, for why else would it make you such a rich gift?" The Elder rarely spoke. He was a graying man who outlived most of his kin. "Tell us how, so that we may also befriend the sea and receive its bounty."

"I sing," said Tralgar. "When I am fishing, I sing to the sea about its beauty, its color, its depth, its treasures."

"Then we shall sing, too," said the Elder. "We shall praise the sea for its gifts that help us live."

There had been five passings of the sun and one rain since the Elder made his proclamation. Tralgar was unaffected for he continued to do what was merely natural to him. He fished the right spots and continued to harvest the bounty of the sea. Not many other fishermen had the same luck as he, even after they began to sing. At the next village meeting, Tralgar was asked to explain.

"I do not know why your catch does not equal my own," said Tralgar.

"You must know what we are doing differently. We fish the same sea, sing the same songs, yet our bounty continues to be only half of yours," stated Hogthrax, the firelight glinting off his eyes like polished metal.

"Explain to us your day, from inspecting your nets to returning with your catch," proclaimed the Elder. The other clansmen nodded their heads, insisting that Tralgar share his knowledge.

"I wake with the sun as do all of you. I break fast with my kin as do all of you. I prepare myself against the cold and damp with my skins as do all of you. I walk to my boat as do all of you and inspect my lines and nets as do all of you. I make way to my fishing grounds as do all of you. And once there I drop my nets and lines as do all of you. I pass the time with mending and singing as do all of you, and when I retrieve my catch I toss back the largest fish as do all of you." Tralgar was interrupted by the village men.

"We do no such thing!" shouted Hogthrax.

"Why did you not tell us of this before?" shouted Flinix, a short wiry man, bronzed and weathered by the elements as all the rest.

"I thought everyone did as I was taught by my father," said Tralgar, who was beginning to wish he had the same fortune at fishing as everyone else.

"But to toss back the largest of the catch?" questioned Hogthrax.

"As Tralgar does, so shall all of we. It is a sign of respect to offer back to the sea the best of what the sea has offered us."

"This is insane. I will do no such thing!" thundered Hogthrax.

"Then it is you who shall continue to catch the least," replied the Elder.

The clan's meeting turned its attention to other matters that concerned the clan and its wellbeing. The fall harvest and the neighbors to the north were two items discussed without further argument.

Tralgar returned to his kin's house after the meeting. It was late and the sun's sister was high in the sky, three quarters pregnant. His mate and kin were fast asleep when he entered his dwelling, the one he had helped his father build ten summers past. It was made of sturdy logs, packed mud plastered the walls and a thatched roof protected against the elements. It was strong and sturdy and would not need to be rebuilt for another twenty warm seasons as long as he kept it in good repair. He decided the next rebuilding would encompass the original walls, making the house stout and twice as strong. As Tralgar slid under the hides next to his mate, she awoke and asked him of the village meeting. Most women were kept ignorant of the meetings and their decisions, but Tralgar shared with his mate.

"They are still trying to equal my catch," Tralgar said softly. "They are convinced that the sea is alive and must be sung to. They believe that the sea is like a man and must be gifted to."

"Why do they believe these things?" asked his mate. Her name was S'Thera and she was wide of eye and plump of body. A very desirable woman in a village with cold winters.

"The village seeks to imitate me and my fishing. They believe if they sing like I do to the sea and throw back the largest of the catch, the sea will increase its gift to them."

"But you sing for the joy of singing and throw back the largest of the catch as your father taught you. You catch the most fish because you are the best fisherman. No other reason."

"I begin to wonder. Does the sea reward me for my gift of song and the largest of my catch?"

"Just you watch, Tralgar, six times the sun will pass and not one fisherman will equal your catch. Now we must be quiet." S'Thera climbed on top of her mate and began kissing him softly under the hides. The kin around them slept quietly on the floor.

"I have tossed back the largest of my catch for five passings of the sun," began Hogthrax. Too angry to sit around the fire with the rest, he paced back and forth as he spoke. "And my catch has not increased but decreased because I threw back the largest of my catch."

The other fishermen grumbled in agreement. Flinix stood, a little ashamed, with eyes down cast.

"My catch increased these past suns. I sang to the sea and I gave back to it what it gave unto me," stated Flinix somberly. He hated standing out, but he had to share his news.

"Is this so?" inquired the Elder, as he stared into the fire.

"Yes," said Flinix before he sat down. The others looked on him with amazement and resentment.

"Then the sea can hear us."

"The sea cannot hear us," said Tralgar standing up. "I catch the most fish because I am a good fisherman. No other reason."

"Then how do you explain the good fortune of Flinix? Surely the sea has shined upon him," said the Elder.

"And what of the rest? No one else has shared his good fortune save I."

"We shall continue on in this manner, and hopefully your words have not angered the sea."

The setting of the next sun found most of the fishermen returning with their greatest catch yet. Tralgar looked on and shook his head as the men spoke of the sea shining upon them.

"What bothers you, Tralgar?" asked Hogthrax with a grin on his face and more fish than he had ever caught in the boat behind him. "It looks as if the sea is on my side now."

"This is the pattern, not the sea. Before the start of each cold season we always catch more, you fool."

"Watch your tongue Tralgar, before you anger the sea."

"Anger the sea? You speak as if the sea is a man with feelings the same as us. It has tides which you'll think are moods. Storms that you'll think is anger. Calm that

19

you'll believe is peaceful. It is not so." Tralgar stormed off back to his kin's house.

The next sun brought a violent storm, the ferocity of which had never been matched in the Elder's memory. Boats were smashed, roofs torn off, a young man of the clan was pulled out into the sea and drowned.

"It is the fault of Tralgar!" proclaimed Hogthrax, on the following sun, after the storm had broken. "He angered the sea with his foolish talk. He even told me that if the sea were angry we would know by the storms."

"He twists my words," replied Tralgar from the entry stone of his kin's house. The clan surrounded him, angry that he could be the cause of this disaster. "I said that the sea is not a man and that if you thought of it as such you would see storms as anger."

"And did we not have storms last sun?" asked Hogthrax of the clan. The clan murmured in agreement.

"We must make amends with the sea," claimed the Elder. "It is still angry and may decide one storm was not enough to teach respect."

"And what do you suggest, Elder?" asked Tralgar.

"We will give you to the sea."

FAITH

The kitchen hadn't been touched for several days now except to make food or brew a pot of coffee in the French press. The dishes were scattered about on the table, the counters, the stove and in the sink with varying depths of crust forming on them. The store of clean dishes was rapidly diminishing and would soon lead to eating over the sink. By the stereo lay a collection of eclectic music ranging from upbeat a capella to ska to Japanese lounge pop to an ambient space music CD which was still in the player. The smell of ammonia and a litter box full of feces emanated from the bathroom and mixed with the stale spice smoke from a clove cigarette. Andy sat in his oversized chair in the corner of his studio apartment waiting for something to happen. Anything. Just as long as it got him out of his rut.

Reclined in morose composure, he took another drag of a clove cigarette, the same kind he had given up three months earlier after a stern rebuke from a close friend on the stupidity of smoking. Right now Andy didn't care. It was something to do; it occupied his hands which he couldn't use to write. It appeared meaningless to him. The prospects of publishing, the sweet dream, was beginning to sour. He had always had a job or a relationship to blame for his lack of motivation, time or resources, for not writing. But now, with nobody to tell him what to do except himself, this fond pastime for his soul left him confused. He had no one to blame if he failed except for

21

himself. Operating without a safety net high above the unforgiving concrete reality that lay everywhere. He was scared.

Andy sat and stared, the smoke filtered the light around him into a blue-grey haze. A window had been opened, dropping the temperature in the apartment to forty-five degrees; the air coming from it was cold and crisp. He didn't seem to notice. His cats lounged carelessly across his shoulders and lap, happy to have someone home for a change yet aware of their master's mood. He was not usually prone to such moods of melancholy. More often than not he would be singing in the shower, whistling as he typed, and dancing in the confines of the one-room apartment, sending the cats helter-skelter for cover. But his silence was what disturbed them most and spoke to them of his need for comfort. He felt none, for he had lost his faith.

The only thing he drew strength from was his new relationship with René. It was different from any he had ever experienced. Unlike others where he would always give and hardly ever take, he finally understood the importance of considering himself. By sharing more of his self, including his weaknesses, he in turn felt more whole, important and strong; even if he didn't realize it at the moment. He couldn't wait for her return. It was agony to him, the most patient of people. "Maybe everything will be better when she gets back," he thought. But he knew that wouldn't be true. He would find momentary comfort in René's arms, but it was he alone who had to find his faith. Until he regained it he would be miserable.

Beyond the Wall of Sleep

Andy picked up his journal and began writing furiously.

Something is gnawing at my insides.
Gnashing its teeth in defiance.
It needs a pacifier, a rubber teat on which to suck.
The last is worn and mottled.
Maybe I'm just going sane.
Slowly stepping up to everyone else's reality
where dreams are only dreams,
fancies of children who are no more.
Dull spirits with lifeless expressions.
Pretend for a moment that you know nothing.
Not your name.
Not your occupation.
Not where you live, your loved ones or relatives.
Not your restless past or dreams of your future.
Imagine that all you are is you as you are.
How do you validate an existence which has no meaning?
How do you validate a life that has no soul?
You can't.
That's why you must believe.
Why you must dream.
Why you must have faith.
Why you must love.
For without those, what are you?

He had finally written the last page of a journal that took him two and a half years to complete. Andy wondered for a moment why it took a year longer than most of his journals, then shelved it next to the rest of his works. Tomorrow he would search for his new journal. Something in which to collect his thoughts like pressed flowers. For now he contemplated his mood and whether it could be contributed to the great number of poems he read on his flight back from Pennsylvania. "Poe and Percy Shelley could do that to anyone," he mentioned to himself, but knew they were only a catalyst for something deeper.

The journal he found was beautifully handmade with blank paper and a marbleized cover. Squarish, it seemed to suit his mood. The purple and gold swirls on the cover played in his mind. What would he write? What would happen next? He did not know, but somehow his life was transformed into those blank virgin pages with endless opportunities and unforeseen turns.

SOLACE

Rising

Jonathan Xavier Quid awoke with a start. Something was terribly wrong. Rolling out of bed and wrapping a bed sheet about his waist, he made his way over to the window. Vast it was, extending from side to side and floor to ceiling. It was more like a wall of glass than a window which overlooked the cascade range. Black venetian blinds let the sunlight trickle through in small diagonal slats, illuminating the dust which hung in the air, thick and choking as if in a mine shaft. He pulled the drawstring down in one sharp movement, letting the sunlight burst forth in torrents.

It was rising

Something pulled from within as Jonathan gazed into the sun. "My god, what will happen to me?" he half whispered to himself. Pivoting on the ball of his foot, he sent a splinter from the hardwood floor deep into his tender flesh. No reaction. The sunlight warmed his naked back. Dropping the sheet, John stepped gingerly out of its supplicating embrace and made his way over to his desk.

No photos or snapshots graced this impressive oaken structure nor mementos or useless boredom gizmos. All that rested on the desk was a sterling silver ballpoint pen poised for official action. Pulling out the top center drawer completely, he overturned it above his desk. The contents spilled out, and a single number two pencil landed on its eraser and launched itself off the desk, completing three full somersaults before clattering to rest on the floor. Countless pens, paperclips, thumbtacks, two sticks of Dentine, a manila folder, a few office doohickies that defy descriptions and names, a gram of coke, and two photos, one of himself at Yale in cap and gown with his arm extending to the bottom left of the frame, the other of a bird in flight blurred beyond recognition.

John stirred the mess with his hands in a counter-clockwise motion while it stewed in his mind. A single stray staple wedged itself under the fingernail of his right ring finger as he raked everything onto the floor. Jonathan did not wince.

Rising yet rising still

Now standing in front of his dresser, Jonathan addressed himself in the mirror. "Who are you?" he asked, demandingly leaning forward and wrapping his hands around the dresser. "What are you?"

"Give me a moment to contemplate what I am!" he shouted.

"...what I am," shouted back Echo.

Lost in the clouds

Jonathan reached for his Perry Ellis wallet that rested in a clean crystal ashtray on the dresser, opened it, and pulled out a State of California driver's license from among the countless credit cards and health club memberships. "I am Jonathan Xavier Quid, a licensed motor vehicle operator in the state of California. Because I am senior vice president at the company and the best lawyers were provided for me to prove I was in full capacity of my faculties the night of the accident, there was no guilty verdict."

Dissolving into the ether

"Verdict . . ." whispered Echo.

Something pulled from deep within as Jonathan gazed into the sun. Slumping to the floor he half whispered to himself, "My God, what will happen to me?"

He stayed like that, naked on the floor curled into a ball, for a very long time.

Jonathan awoke four days later with a yawning empty feeling in his gut that went beyond hunger. It was as if something had been entirely removed from him that no manner of consumption could fill. Twenty-three messages filled his answering machine. He erased them all without listening to them. He knew what they would say.

Gorging himself on food and drink, he tried to fill the emptiness he felt inside. Even when he had eaten to the point of vomiting, the hollowness still consumed him. He dated women who said they felt shut out, closed off, and distanced by him. He went to clubs with pals from work, but found no solace in their company either.

One day, he stepped from the curb into the path of an oncoming car. He had ceased to move within the world. The world was now moving past him. A moment before he was struck by the car, he was pulled back by a stranger who looked vaguely familiar. Jonathan knelt and wept at the corner. When he looked back up, the man who saved him was gone, clouds gathered overhead and the rain began to fall.

Jonathan continued to sob and weep, cursing himself and his fear for at that moment he realized he was afraid to die. He was afraid to die because he had no soul.

Ava Bryne

Closing the door with a caress, he stepped out quietly to make sure she did not awake. He didn't know how to leave her. He also didn't know why he was leaving her. Something was "not right" and this was the only thing that made some semblance of sense to him. The pain was too great. To him, the best way was to slip out quietly. No tears, no good-byes, just a memory of what was.

Under the soft sheets she awakes and gradually realizes he is gone. Anger fills her heart. How could he do this? Why did he do this? What was he afraid of? The answers were with him, and he was gone. She strides over to the mirror and gazes deeply, looking into her soul to ask "Why?" Why? To find the answers she wished so desperately to find.

He ran down the street, tears flooding his eyes. The message was unclear in his tight-fisted gut. With each step he became weaker, his vision more blurred. Her image repeatedly came back to him as the sun rose and the train pulled into the station.

In the mirror, she grasps at images she wishes she could continue to live with. Saturday morning tea with him to keep her warm. Strolls in the park. A loving touch and a supporting glance. He was all to her and she wanted him back. Needed him back.

The train stopped, doors opened. He hesitated briefly and then stepped on. Not looking back. Eyes forward. Travel always reminded him of the future because he was moving toward it and didn't know who or what it held.

She holds tight to the frame of her vanity mirror, her knuckles turning white, blood rushing away from the anger. Too much heartache and too much pain was in that mirror, in which she sees her memories float past. She pulls the mirror out of its support and smashes it against the bureau top. A million shards of existence sparkle before her, and a red river pours forth from her neck into it.

The train moved on through the land. Rails conquered it long ago and now the passive earth yielded to the great metal giant. Soaring along. The man could only face forward in the compartment. Facing backwards made him nauseous. Across from him was an old man. Wrinkles had their way with his face and the spectacles he wore sunk deep into his nose. He knew. The old man looked at him and knew.

"You're a blind man running passionately toward a cliff," said the old man.

"How do you know?" he asked.

"Why do you think I'm facing backwards?" replied the old man.

AN INTERVIEW WITH GOD

The secretary sat across from me with her legs crossed, causing her hip-hugging yellow knit skirt to slip, showing just a bit too much thigh for me to continue rational thought. She spoke and my eyes traveled to her lips.

"Here are your travel arrangements for you and your family. . ." she rifled through some more papers, ". . . and your brochure. I hope you have a wonderful time, I've been there several times myself."

Finally achieving eye contact with her after climbing her body with my eyes, I asked, "What did you think of it?" Breathing hard with the climb I awaited her response.

The secretary's auburn hair cascaded over her left shoulder and as she responded she adjusted her glasses on a thimble she called a nose. "It's a lot like an amusement park, you can do anything, go anywhere and be anyone. Just decide what you want early on; that way you don't get rushed by the end of your stay." She passed the papers to me causing me to turn my mental energies toward receiving them and away from undressing her in my mind; the worst part was that my hand had just reached the front clasp on her bra. It was black. "And by the way," the secretary added, "here is your birth visa. It looks like you are going to be an Aquarius."

"Sounds absolutely delightful. Anything else?"

"No, just your interview with God. Are you

ready?" She asked with a hint of smile hanging on her lips.

"I believe so," I replied with an edge of uncertainty.

"Well, good luck," and as an afterthought she added, "and have a nice life."

"I'll be sure to," I replied as I rose from my plush chair and shook souls with the secretary. We both blushed not only at the thoughts I had but at hers, too. She imagined I was wearing a pair of polka-dot boxer-shorts.

I left the small office and made my way down the vast ethereal hallway towards God's office. I wonder if this is how I will feel in the first grade when I am sent to the principal's office? I mused. Meanwhile my footsteps echoed down the hallway and raced back to me, but the doorway at the end continued to be as far away as ever. I passed star charts, visions of the universe and essences of beings as I made my way closer, yet not closer, to the door. "I wonder if he did this on purpose?" I said aloud and chuckled, but it was cut off by an immense dark mahogany door. In the center of the door rested a plaque created of pure light. In giant capital letters that commanded great respect and awe, it read

GOD .

Below it in more solemn characters and in parentheses was the request

(Please knock),

and to the right of the door was a small wastebasket created of a silver mesh with a sign from God.

Leave your troubles at the door.
Thank you,
God

I knocked, a lifeless thud of a knock devoid of any strength compared to that of the Creator. There was no answer. I knocked again but the sound was cut off by a voice. A voice which was neither male nor female, young nor old, but was entirely warm, compassionate and wise; this voice said "Enter." I did and saw God. God was sitting behind a large desk built of the same dark mahogany as the door, which commanded great respect for whoever sat behind it. The grain was a beautiful bird's-eye, highly polished and so smooth that I could see my own reflection in it and understand the history of the tree from which it had been cut. Meanwhile, behind the desk sat God. To say what God looked like would not even do justice to its appearance. To say that God radiated pure love, kindness, beauty and truth would not even begin to flatter it. To say that God shown brighter than ten-thousand stars going supernova would still fall short by 83 light years. God defies description, but God's desk does not.

"Take a seat and please close your mouth," God said in that warm voice. "I'm a very busy person." I took a seat on another plush red velvet chair and failed to say anything, but managed to close my mouth, which had been agape with awe. "So this is your first time going to Earth, eh?" I nodded my head in response as words continued to fail me. "It says here that you have been working in the Akashic Records. What did you think of it?"

I found words, they were lying in a small red

bucket at my feet. "It's quite a job, lots of updating and filing, only one regular patron though. His name is Edgar Cayce, he keeps me busy looking up records on Jesus and Atlantis. He's given me a good idea as to what Earth is like and I am looking forward to my incarnation."

"I am sure that you will find Earth quite exciting; my son Jesus did," God stated in that voice that is still beyond description.

"Great, wow, you're okaying my birth visa? Oh joyous rapture!"

"Whoa, whoa! Hold it down, we have to discuss a few things first."

"Like what I'm supposed to learn?" I asked and grew a little smaller.

"Yes, that's a start."

"Ok, how about commitment, honesty and I'll throw in sharing for good measure." As I said these words, three spheres of silver light came into existence above God's beautiful mahogany desk. I finally noticed a time and space chart with my name on it on top of God's desk and these spheres hovered above times in the life I was about to enter on Earth.

"That sounds good, but you are leaving out patience for yourself . . ." another silver sphere appeared above the desk "and for others," then split in half. "as well as the many forms of love." A golden sphere appeared with a rainbow of satellite spheres around it. "You are also going to have to master relationships if you plan to meet up with the rest of your family on Earth." God paused and the room shook with the silence. "You are going with family, are you not?"

"Yes, yes with five others," I stuttered.

"Good." God held a clenched fist above the time/space chart. "Five, right?"

"Yes." God opened the fist and in the weathered palm five blue lights rested. "When will I meet them?"

"Well, you can't know your whole destiny," God said with a grin that filled the universe.

"Destiny?" I exclaimed incredulously, "I thought my package included free will! The secretary showed me the brochure!"

"Of course it does, but it grants you free will to screw up if you choose to."

"Oh," I replied with general dismay.

"Any questions? I have some evolution to attend to on Pluto." It appeared that God was wrapping up the interview.

"Yes, I have one question. How do you feel? Some souls say you get depressed because everything you create dies."

"I feel great; I could use a back rub, but that is beside the point. It doesn't bother me that everything I create dies because nothing ever really dies. When you get to Earth you will learn this."

"I am looking forward to it," I said in earnest.

"Well good! Good! It looks as though you are going to learn a great deal, especially since Earth is a crash course on life."

The Dead Travel Fast

Unsightly colors, purple in hue, envelop young Arthur Drew in a warmth incomparable to the soft downy bed he knew in a small New England town. Drawn, pulled upwards and outwards, terminating this earth-bound existence for another existence far more grand. Arthur travels toward what is always there, waiting for each man, woman and child to draw their last breath. A tunnel to the future and a journey through the past are the first obstacles of Arthur's repass.

As a child he saw to the destruction of flies in fiery flames. Paralyzed by tweezers, wings thoughtlessly removed, the blue azure body begins to fume. A plume of black smoke wisps gently to his nose as a point of the sun makes the fly glow. His gaze was amazed at their spontaneous doom with the power of the sun and a new magnifying glass.

At twelve, knickknacks were the facts of his sister's distress. Her prized precious joys, pewter in hue, just wouldn't do for young Arthur Drew. He saw fit to their flight from two stories high into a pricker bush that happened to be close by.

Now poor Arthur Drew, close to the end, begins to worry about the beginning of his end. "Surely I must have done just one thing right." So he stood and he thought with all of his might at what that one thing might have been.

On Mother's Day at age fourteen, he ruined a

garden in night unseen to deliver his mom a noble deed, a bouquet of tulips and pretty weeds.

Age fifteen was all the worse; could his life have been a curse? Caught cheating on a test and called the teacher's pest was just an appetizer for all the rest.

But up ahead, what could that be? A precious act? A noble deed? Driving at speeds unrestrained, Arthur drove along the main. When all of a sudden with no type of warning a small fuzzy squirrel jumped into his path. He swerved to the left and then to the right, right into an oncoming tree.

"No matter how great and no matter how small, the good you do saves us all," a voice of mighty proportions intoned. So this was the act that let Arthur pass from this world into the next.

For the dead travel quick
in the blink of an eye
a loose tongue can bring knowledge
and random thoughts make them fly.

THE VOICE

"Boo."

I listened closely. There was no follow-up to the spectral admission. Once and that was all. Not the cry of a banshee or the wailings of a lost soul but "boo." A friendly prank if ever there was one. I had no idea that Francis existed before last night and after a quick visit that left me spellbound, I had no further recourse to follow but to think about him. I guess he was always there, lurking behind me or around, but I never noticed. But why now? What had changed to give me the ability to hear him or communicate? I know not.

The fire blazed away in the hearth and my cat Poe was quietly purring and licking himself.

"Boo."

I could have sworn I heard it again. I looked up from my book which I hadn't been able to concentrate on since the first "boo." "Where are you?" I demanded. The fire crackled, Poe looked at me expectantly. I paced around the room, my bare feet padding softly on the oriental rug. "I know you are here. You cannot just say "boo" and leave it at that. If you are a spectre from beyond the grave you could at least do me the favor of imparting me with insights from the afterlife." Silence. Worse than silence: no response. I suddenly felt observed, objectified, measured and weighed to the last inch and ounce. Studied and contemplated like a scientific anomaly. "This is not fair.

Not in the least. Not one mote or speck of this reeks of fairness. SPEAK!"

"And what is it you would have me say?" replied the disembodied voice. It rang of age and wisdom, old wood and the wind through trees. I was aghast. It spoke. Until this moment I had fancied I was playing myself for a lark, scaring myself with a raven of sorts, but this was unexpected and horrifying. I turned up the lamp. I found it suddenly necessary to illuminate every corner, nook and cranny of the room, lest it hide something. But the voice, despite the light, remained. "I will talk now."

"No you won't," I stated. I hadn't the nerve to converse with the ether.

"But you summoned me."

"I did no such thing. You said 'boo'."

"It was merely an attempt to attract your attention. Which it did for afterward you commanded me to speak."

"I did no. . ." I slumped into my chair with the realization of what I had done. Truly, no man with humors well balanced would call out to a voice he heard through the crackling of the fire and demand it make its presence known. "Get out!"

"But don't you wish to know?"

"No! . . . Know what?"

"What I know."

"Which is."

"What lies beyond the wall of sleep."

"There is no wall."

"Only the wall you create."

"What manner of riddles do you employ in your attempt to pray on my confusion?"

"None whatsoever. The walls are yours to build and yours to tear down."

"And what walls are those?"

"The ones that keep you from life, from living, from love unbridled."

Despite the radiant warmth of the fire I pulled a quilt up around my body, which had grown quite suddenly cold.

"Why don't you leave me?"

"I cannot."

"Why?" I pleaded. "Why can't you leave me in peace?"

"Because I am part of you."

The room grew silent, the fire died down and one by one the candles and lamps burned themselves out before the coming of the dawn. I was awake for it all and afraid of myself.

THE POETRY

TO MY MUSE

Muse, leave me not right now
in my moment of need.
Stay up late with me.
Use me until my hand cramps with arthritic pain
and I must bathe it in quick warm water and salts.
Your visits are few and far between.
Leave your number
so I might visit you for a change,
buzz inside your head
and make love with your soul.
Let **you** put it in words,
put it on paper,
on canvas,
on stage,
into someone's mind.
Let me be the muse
and dance in your thoughts for a change,
chasing my footprints
trying to get it all down fore they disappear
back into the shifting sands of the mind.
Quick they are, quicker more are you.
The path leads to the greatest glory,
the mother lode,
and if the vision is
great enough,
clear enough,
large enough,
a glimpse might be all it takes
to understand
everything.

PĬN

You take a razor sharp pin
and prick my subconscious.
I flow with you.

PSYCHE'S POOL

The breath of the stars rests lightly upon my neck
as I stare deeply into the pool of water
at the reflection of a man I thought I knew.
Looking harder,
I fall into the reflection of my own eye's reflection
and a dark void surrounds me.
Time fails to pass
until a voice carries across the still water.
"Cry baby cry
into the cold dark sky,
the night is not a comforting blanket."
"It is not in the night sky that I seek my comfort
but in the realization of who I am,"
I call back to the voice.
A loon cries and I jerk back
finding myself once again
kneeling at the edge of the pool,
not sure of why I was there,
who I was
or what I was doing.

WANDERING

In the seditious wanderings
of an innocent Jew
through the desert of his mind
he finds the courage to let go
and be carried upon the wind
He brings me to a land
bordering on reality
lets me see my dreams
keys to a lesson never learned
Give up the dead to resurrection
and lie here in a shallow grave
I grieve not for who I am
but for what I might become
Forget not the story
of those who left before you
Did they return?
Will you?
What has fate in store
to give, buy, purchase or lease?
It is not yours to own freely
but to take and cherish and
share.

SECRET

A secret kept is a promise good
and a friendship kept is a wondrous thing.
For who can pass the judge of experience
and keep a friend in tow
might one day outgrow that friend
who they once did know.

UNVEILED

Look unto me with eyes unveiled
see what there is to see
It is not hidden behind clouds
of lies and deceit
It has one name and that is love
There is no more
there is no less
it is great in its simplest form
Love
all that you can

WHERE THE FUTURE LIES

Moving forward not back to where you began
the future expands even further
the more you move toward it.
If you catch up to it
you can pass it
and redirect
where it is going in the first place.
Everything is fated but nothing has happened yet.
That's free will
that's what you get for being alive
and being human
you stupid shit.
Don't fuck with it by being bored.
Get down and dirty,
get your hands wet
and gunk under your nails.
Dig, find, retrieve what has been lost
reclaim what is yours by right
and share it with the world.
It can only happen once.
This is your chance to make it happen for you.
Go on to the rest of your life.

SCHMA

Yah, yah, yah
shit, shit, shit
Schma, schma, schma
This is what comes out of a lot of people's mouths.
Fortunately I am friends with a lot of people
who have more to say than this.
But from time to time
and even I am guilty of this
all I hear is
Yah, yah, yah
shit, shit, shit
Schma, schma, schma
when their mouths open up.
Get real!
Speak the truth that lays heavily upon your mind.

PISS

Piss Piss
piss in a pot
I should be happy
cause that's all I got.
Piss Piss
piss in a pot
I should be angry
cause that's all I got.

R. Andrew Heidel

TO SEE GOD IT DOES NOT TAKE THE EYES OF AN ANGEL

A friend and I
traded eyes yesterday
she took a look around
and smiled at what she saw
but everything I looked at
I felt hatred and disgust for
I said may I have my eyes back now?
She said "no" and ran away
I hated what I saw in her
I hated what I saw in me
But wait, I used to have these eyes
her eyes,
my eyes,
but I realized
god was everywhere
and in everything
so I looked for god again
and slowly
I began to see god in everything
and smiled at what I saw.

OVER TEA WITH INGRID

What's on your mind? asks she
Your lips, answers he
My lips where? asks she
Upon my lips, answers he
But what is it you want? asks she
To follow my heart, answers he
Where does your heart lead? asks she
To you, answers he

HER

I look at her and see a child
she is innocent in her ways
she says the ocean is her thoughts
and the birds are in her ears.
I believe her when she says this.
I cannot help but to.
I believe it is so.

HOW I ENVY YOUR ABANDON

You are liquid in your being
flowing with the tides
of music's pulsing rhythm
and life's subtle cycle
You are liquid in your being
by letting go
and plunging into the everything
How I envy your abandon

A FLOWER

A flower picked at its peak of beauty
fresh fragrant and full of color
But as time goes by
this thing of beauty
bestowed as a gift of love
begins to fade and wilt.
Why not place the flower
in an airless jar
preserving it in ageless beauty?
A beauty that does not age or fade
is lost in time
not part of this world
and always untouchable.
The beauty that ages
becomes all the more cherished
when you press it to your heart.

GABRIELLE'S PASSION

Shackles, they rubbed her ankles raw
Cutting, deep into her flesh
Circular mandates kept her in line

"Move!" shouted the driver
Sneering, his chapped lips pulled tight
across a row of rotting yellow teeth

Rising still, pushing pulsing
An aura of emotion surrounds her body
Rush! Power complete
Emotion
Emitting emoting, condensing, creating

She clenches a fist
Opens it, clenches it, opens it once again

That was, this is
Clenches. Opens. Her mind's eye opens
Open, influx, pulsing, breathing
Close, oppress, suffering, pleading
Bleeding

Open, yes. Open
She casts off the shackles.

R. Andrew Heidel

EPITAPH

Friend, unto you I depart this, my life's understanding of matters indescribable: love, friendship, the soul, passion, art. These merits of life, unrecognizable unless truly valued, imbue the bearer with a greatness not unlike the fragrance of a flower. It emanates from within and attracts from without and with the same wherewithal brings one to where they have to be.